THE WIZARD
of
OZ

INTRODUCTION
by Margaret Hamilton

"There's no place like home."

Those were the magic words Dorothy repeated over and over to escape from the mystical, ofttimes terrifying Land of Oz back to Kansas.

More importantly, that was the ever so simple truth author L. Frank Baum used to reach out and touch the hearts of readers and play audiences in the early 20th century, then movie goers in the 1940's and finally generations of television viewers from the 1950's on. Home is very, very special to us all. Especially a childhood home like Dorothy's. It means love and safety and comfort and pets and back-yards and Mom. Wherever we go in life, whenever we run into troubles — as did Dorothy — we instinctively think of home and long to escape there.

That is the message of the *Wizard of Oz*. That is what makes it so endearing a story to us all.

I think it is significant that when Wizard first came out as a movie in 1939, both critics and audiences gave it passing but not overly enthusiastic marks. It was not until the 1950's, when the film began to be seen on television that *Oz* caught on. I think that's because it was being seen in the home. Families gathered. Curtains were drawn. Children snuggled down in parent's laps. Grandparents thought of days long ago. Popcorn and cookies were passed. Dogs curled up under foot. The world, with all its troubles, was shut out for a brief hour or so. Dorothy ran away from home, couldn't get back, was whisked off to Oz, made friends, triumphed against evil, was betrayed and then despaired that home was lost forever. Suddenly, Glinda, the Good Witch of the South, sends her home with those five precious words: "There's no place like home."

Who can keep a dry eye, whether three or 93?

Wise men tell us we can't go home. But, Dorothy did. And, she did it for all of us. That's why *Oz* is so special...and will remain so as long as man is born and reared in a home.

Margaret B. Hamilton.

This edition is dedicated to Margaret Hamilton for her pivotal roll in bringing the magic of *OZ* into the hearts and minds of so many. The memories of her special magic will live on as long as we all believe in fantasy and dreams.

Mother had two loves: children and acting.

She taught nursery school, before landing her first role on Broadway. Her commitment to the education of children, especially small children, ran very deep.

Thus, while Mother enjoyed immensely her role of the Wicked Witch of the West, she constantly worried about its impact on small children. She always feared her portrayal was too realistic — too "scary" as she would say. She feared children would have difficulty understanding that the "Wizard" and the "Witch" were just make-believe. I remember countless times, her stooping, in the midst of signing an autograph, to reassure a child that the Witch, her long nose and all that green make-up were just fantasy. She would remind both parent and child, always with a twinkle, that the character up on the screen was really just a nice lady who, by the way, had a son of her own.

She did this in the 1940's, 1950's, 1960's, 1970's and 1980's. Children, with whom she talked early on, would bring back their children for reassurance. In the last years it was often grandchildren!

She wrote the introduction to this edition of "Wizard" just before she died in May 1985. As she stressed, the theme of all of us wanting to go home is central to "Wizard". But, what is basic to that yearning, I'm sure she would argue, is the child in us. She loved that quality of the child as she loved all children.

She would be greatly honored that this book is dedicated to her. But, knowing Mom, she would probably protest that this book really belongs to the children — all the children who have and will continue to thrill, wide-eyed, to the *Wizard of Oz*.

Hamilton W. Meserve

THE WIZARD
of
OZ

By L. Frank Baum

Illustrated by Greg Hildebrandt

The Unicorn Publishing House
New Jersey

Designed by Jean L. Scrocco.
Edited by Heidi K. L. Corso.
Printed in Korea through
Creative Graphics International, New York, NY.
Typography by L&B Typography of N.Y.C.
Reproduction Photography by The Color Wheel, New York, NY.

♦ ♦ ♦ ♦ ♦

♦ ♦ ♦ ♦ ♦

Distributed in Canada by Doubleday Canada, Toronto, ON

♦ ♦ ♦ ♦ ♦

Special thanks to Yoh Jinno, and the entire Unicorn staff.

♦ ♦ ♦ ♦ ♦

Printing History   10   9   8   7   6   5   4   3   2   1

♦ ♦ ♦ ♦ ♦

Library of Congress Cataloging-in-Publication Data

Baum, L. Frank (Lyman Frank), 1856-1919.
The Wizard of Oz.

Summary: After a cyclone transports her to the land of Oz,
Dorothy must seek out the great wizard in order
to return to Kansas.

(1. Fantasy)   I. Hildebrandt, Greg, ill.   II. Title.
PZ7.B327Wi   1988   [Fic]   87-30182
ISBN 0-88101-076-6

Additional Classic and Contemporary Editions
Richly Illustrated in
This Little Unicorn Series:

ANTIQUE FAIRY TALES

PINOCCHIO

HEIDI

PETER PAN

CAST OF CHARACTERS

Michael Paglia • The Wizard
Dana Devins • Dorothy
Evelyn Enteman • Aunt Em
Greg Hildebrandt • Uncle Henry
Germaine Hildebrandt • The Good Witch
Jean Scrocco • The Wicked Witch; Oz as a beautiful lady
Gene O'Brien • Soldier (The Army of Oz); Flying Monkeys
Michael Resnick • Guardian of the Gates
Heidi Corso • Glinda
Joyce Dickson • Dancing Munchkin; Oz Citizen
Michael Dickson • Dancing Munchkin; Oz Citizen
Penny Sergeff • Munchkin Grandmother; Oz Citizen
Robbie McCann • Munchkin; Oz Citizen
Stephanie Peters • Munchkin Child; Oz Citizen
Joey Martinez • Bog
Mary Hildebrandt • Bog's Wife
Joseph Scrocco, Sr. • Oz Citizen
Jeannie Scrocco • Oz Citizen
Heather Hawes • Oz Citizen; Winkie
Joan Foley • Oz Citizen
Judy McCann • Oz Citizen
Bill McGuire • Oz Citizen
Gregory Hildebrandt • Oz Citizen
Laura Hildebrandt • Oz Citizen
Delfino Falciani • Winkie
Bob Smith • Winkie
Karen White • Winkie

Toto • Compliments of:
Second Chance Pet Adoption League

Models Made by Greg Hildebrandt for:
Scarecrow
Tin Man
Lion

LIST OF ILLUSTRATIONS

1. Dorothy at home in Kansas
2. The Cyclone
3. The Good Witch gives Dorothy the silver shoes
4. The Munchkin party
5. Dorothy meets the Scarecrow
6. Dorothy and the Scarecrow find the Tin Woodman
7. The Cowardly Lion sends the Scarecrow spinning
8. The Kalidahs attack
9. Stuck fast in the mud
10. The deadly poppy field
11. The mice rescue the Lion
12. The Emerald City on the horizon
13. Inside the gates of Oz
14. Oz, the Great and Terrible
15. The Scarecrow enters the great throne room
16. The Wicked Witch of the West
17. The Scarecrow slays the crows
18. The Wicked Witch uses the charm of the Golden Cap
19. The Wicked Witch threatens Dorothy
20. Dorothy melts the Wicked Witch
21. Toto discovers the secret of Oz
22. The Tin Woodman's heart
23. The balloon is launched
24. The soldier with the green whiskers
25. Attacked by the fighting trees
26. Dorothy and the China Clown
27. The Hammer-Heads
28. Glinda's ruby throne room
29. Dorothy says goodbye
30. Home again

THE WIZARD
of
OZ

Dorothy lived in the midst of the great Kansas prairies, with her Uncle Henry and Aunt Em. Their house was one room, with no garret at all, and no cellar, except a small hole dug in the ground, called a cyclone cellar, where the family could go in case one of those great whirlwinds arose.

When Dorothy looked ouside of the house, she could see nothing but the great gray prairie on every side. The sun and the wind had baked the land into a gray mass with little cracks running through it. The grass was gray, for the sun had burned the tops of the long blades. The paint of the house had worn away, until the house was as gray as everything else.

Aunt Em had come there when she was a young, pretty wife. The sun and wind had changed her, too. They had taken the sparkle from her eyes and left them a sober gray. She was thin and gaunt, and never smiled now.

Uncle Henry was gray also, from his long beard to his rough boots, and he looked stern and solemn, and rarely spoke.

It was Toto that saved Dorothy from growing as gray as her other surroundings. Toto was a little black dog with long silky hair who played all day long, and he was Dorothy's only friend.

Today, however, they were not playing. Uncle Henry was looking up anxiously at the sky. Suddenly, he said, "There's a cyclone coming, Em. I'll go look after the stock." Then he ran towards the sheds where the cows and horses were kept.

Aunt Em dropped her work and came to the door. One glance told her of the danger close at hand. "Quick, Dorothy!" she screamed, "run for the cellar!"

Toto jumped out of Dorothy's arms and hid under the bed, and the little girl started to get him. Aunt Em, badly frightened, threw open the trap door in the floor and climbed down the ladder into the small dark hole.

Dorothy at home in Kansas

Dorothy caught Toto at last, and started to follow her aunt. When she was halfway across the room there came a great shriek from the wind, and the house shook so hard that she sat down suddenly on the floor.

A strange thing then happened.

The house whirled around two or three times and then rose slowly through the air. Dorothy felt as if she were going up in a balloon. It rose to the top of the cyclone and there it remained, and was carried miles and miles away as easily as you can carry a feather.

It was very dark and the wind howled horribly around her, but Dorothy found she was riding quite easily. After the first few whirls around, she felt as if she were being rocked gently, like a baby in the cradle.

Hour after hour passed away. Slowly Dorothy got over her fright, but she felt quite lonely. At first she wondered if she would be dashed to pieces if the house fell again; but as the hours passed and nothing terrible happened, she resolved to wait calmly and see what the future would bring. At last she lay down on her bed and fell fast asleep.

The Cyclone

She was awakened by a bump and realized that the cyclone had set the house down. Dorothy ran to the door and looked out. The house was in the midst of a beautiful country. All about her were trees bearing rich and luscious fruits, patches of emerald green grass, colorful flowers, and birds with brilliant plumage.

Then she noticed coming toward her a group of very strange people. There were three men who were about as tall as Dorothy, and an old woman in white. They all wore tall pointed hats with bells around the brim that tinkled sweetly as they moved.

"I am the Good Witch of the North," said the old woman, "and I welcome you to the land of Oz. You are a heroine, for when your house fell, it landed on the Wicked Witch of the East, and set the Munchkins free from bondage. Now there is only one wicked witch left in all the land: the Wicked Witch of the West."

Dorothy looked where the Witch pointed. Underneath her house were two feet sticking out, shod in Silver Shoes. One of the Munchkins handed the shoes to the Witch, and she gave them to Dorothy. "They are yours; there is a charm connected with these shoes," the little woman said, "but what it is, I do not know."

Dorothy asked if the charm might help her to go home.

The Good Witch gives Dorothy the silver shoes

"The land of Oz is surrounded by a great desert," said the Witch. "The only one who could help you home is the Great Wizard, Oz, in the Emerald City. He is a great Wizard who can take any form he wishes. It is a long journey, but the road is paved with yellow brick." She kissed Dorothy gently on the forehead. Where her lips touched left a shining mark. "I have given you my kiss, and no one will dare injure a person who has been kissed by the Witch of the North. Good-bye, my dear." The three Munchkins bowed to Dorothy and walked away. The Witch smiled and disappeared.

Dorothy went into the house and packed some bread in a basket. She put on a clean gingham dress, and then looked at her worn shoes. "These will never do for a long journey, Toto," she said. She tried on the silver slippers and found that they fit her, so she put them on and began her journey.

She found the country very pretty as she walked. The houses of the Munchkins were very odd looking, as they were all round. All were painted blue, for in that country, blue was the favorite color. Toward evening, when Dorothy grew tired, she stopped at a large house. There was a party on the lawn, and the Munchkins greeted Dorothy, and invited her to pass the night with them.

The Munchkin party

Dorothy agreed, and spent a happy night. The next morning she bade her new friends good-bye and again started walking down the yellow brick road. When she had gone several miles, she sat down on a fence and looked up at a Scarecrow, who was propped up on a pole. He was dressed in an old suit of Munchkin clothes and wore an old pointed hat. He also wore old boots with blue tops.

As Dorothy looked into the queer painted face of the Scarecrow, she was suprised to see one of the eyes wink at her.

"Good day," said the Scarecrow, in a rather husky voice.

"Good day," returned Dorothy in surprise. "Can't you get down from there?"

"No," said the Scarecrow, "for this pole is stuck up my back. If you could take me down I would be much obliged to you."

Dorothy lifted the straw man off the pole. "My name is Dorothy," she said "and I am going to the Emerald City to ask the great Wizard of Oz to send me home to Kansas."

"Do you think," asked the Scarecrow, "that the Wizard might give me some brains if I asked? You see, my head is stuffed with straw." Toto sniffed the straw man. "I cannot say," said Dorothy, "but come with me and ask."

Dorothy meets the Scarecrow

They went back to the road, and started walking. Toward evening, they came to a great forest, and spent the night in a deserted cabin.

When Dorothy awoke, she, the Scarecrow and Toto began walking through the forest. Suddenly, Dorothy gave a cry of surprise. In front of them stood a man made entirely of tin. He stood quite still, as if he could not stir at all.

"Please get an oil can and oil my joints," said the tin man, "for they are rusted so badly, I can't move at all."

Dorothy remembered seeing an oil can in the cabin, so she ran back and got it. Then she oiled the tin man's joints until he could move again.

"My name is Dorothy," she said, when she finished. "We are going to see the Wizard of Oz. I'm going to ask him to send me home, and the Scarecrow is going to ask him for some brains."

"Do you think he would give me a heart?" asked the tin man. "You see, the tinsmith forgot to give me one."

"Why I suppose he could," said Dorothy. "It would be as easy as giving the Scarecrow some brains."

"Come along," said the Scarcrow, heartily.

Dorothy and the Scarecrow find the Tin Woodman

As the companions traveled, the forest got deeper and gloomier. From behind the trees came deep growls. These sounds made the little girl's heart beat fast.

Suddenly, a huge Lion leapt out from a tree and bounded in the road. With one blow from his paw, he sent the Scarecrow spinning over and over. Then he struck the Tin Woodman with his sharp claws, but to the Lion's surprise, he could make no impression on the tin, although the Woodman fell over in the road and lay still.

Little Toto ran forward barking and the Lion opened his mouth to bite him. Dorothy ran forward, heedless of the danger and slapped the Lion on the nose, as hard as she could.

"I didn't bite him," said the Lion, rubbing his nose. "You didn't have to hit me."

"You're nothing but a big coward," said Dorothy.

"I know," said the Lion, "and it makes me so unhappy."

"Why don't you come with us to see the Wizard of Oz?" asked Dorothy. "Perhaps he could give you courage."

"Perhaps I will," said the Lion. "Life is simply unbearable without a bit of courage."

The Cowardly Lion sends the Scarecrow spinning

The forest got thicker as the party walked on. To add to their discomfort, they heard strange noises in the depths of the forest, and the Lion whispered to them that it was in this part of the country that the Kalidahs lived.

"What are Kalidahs?" asked the little girl.

"They are monstrous beasts with bodies like bears and heads like tigers. They have claws so long and sharp that they could tear me in two easily. I'm terribly afraid of the Kalidahs."

As they walked, the group came to a wide ravine. It was too far to jump, so the Woodman chopped down a tree which fell across the gulf. They had just started to cross this queer bridge when they heard a roar. To their horror they saw running toward them two beasts with bodies like bears and heads like tigers.

"They are the Kalidahs!" cried the Cowardly Lion.

As they got to the other side, the Woodman chopped down the bridge and just as the two Kalidahs were nearly across, the tree fell with a crash into the gulf, carrying the ugly snarling brutes with it. Both were dashed to pieces on the sharp rocks below.

The Kalidahs attack

The travelers walked on anxiously. To their great joy they suddenly came upon a broad river. On the other side of the river, they could see the yellow brick road.

So the Tin Woodman took his axe and began to build a raft. When he finished, they all climbed aboard and the Scarecrow and Tin Woodman used long poles to push the raft through the water.

They got along quite well at first, but suddenly, the Scarecrow's pole stuck fast in the mud. Before he could let go, the raft was swept away and the poor Scarecrow was left clinging to the pole in the middle of the river.

The Lion sprang into the water and, giving the end of his tail to the Woodman to hold, pulled them to shore at last. The party climbed off the raft, and looked out at the river. The Scarecrow was perched on the pole looking very sad and lonely.

His friends did not know what to do, so they sat down on the bank and gazed wistfully at him. Just then, a big stork flew by and asked them what they were doing. Finding out their problem, the stork flew over to the Scarecrow and, lifting him in her great claws, carried him over to his friends. Then the kind stork flew into the air, and was soon out of sight.

Stuck fast in the mud

When the Scarecrow found himself among his friends again, he was so happy that he hugged them all, and sang gaily at every step. They walked along happily looking at the lovely flowers which carpeted the ground. There were big yellow and white blossoms, and beside them great clusters of scarlet poppies which dazzled Dorothy's eyes. As they walked further, there were more and more poppies and less of the other flowers. The spicy scent of the poppies filled the air.

Now it is well known that when there are many of these flowers together, their odor is so powerful that anyone who breathes it falls asleep. If the sleeper is not carried away from the scent of the flowers, he sleeps on forever. But Dorothy did not know this and presently her eyes grew heavy and she felt she must lie down and sleep. Her eyes closed in spite of herself. She forgot where she was and fell fast asleep among the poppies.

Toto had fallen asleep already and lay beside his little mistress. Realizing the danger, the Scarecrow told the Lion to run ahead. Then he and the Tin Woodman picked up Dorothy and Toto and carried them to safety. When they were almost out of the poppy field, they found the Lion sound asleep in the poppies.

The deadly poppy field

"He is too heavy to lift," said the Woodman sadly.

They carried Dorothy and Toto farther, and laid them gently on the ground, far away from the deadly scent of the poppies. Suddenly, the Woodman heard a low growl and saw a great yellow wildcat chasing a little gray field mouse. Raising his axe, he chopped the wildcat's head off.

The little field mouse approached the Woodman and said in a squeaky little voice, "Oh thank you, ever so much, for saving my life. I am the Queen of all of the field mice. Let my subjects repay your brave deed by obeying your slightest wish."

The Scarecrow spoke up quickly. "Perhaps you can help us save our friend, the Lion, who is lying asleep in the poppies. The Woodman can make a cart, and if you would allow us, we could harness all of your subjects to it and they could rescue him."

The Queen gave an order and shortly after, thousands of field mice appeared. Each carried a string and the Scarecrow harnessed them to the wooden cart. At first the little creatures could not move the cart, but when the Scarecrow and Tin Woodman got behind it and pushed, the cart rolled quite easily through the field and out into the fresh air.

The mice rescue the Lion

"If ever you need our assistance again," said the mouse queen, "just come out into a field and call us. We shall come right away to help." Then the mice ran away.

The friends sat down to wait for the Lion to wake up. When he did, they continued traveling down the yellow brick road. The country all around them was green and very pretty.

Soon, they saw a beautiful green city ahead of them. "That must be the Emerald City," said Dorothy. Shortly, they came to the green wall that surrounded the city.

In front of them, at the end of the yellow brick road, was a big gate, studded with emeralds that glittered brilliantly in the sun. There was a bell beside the gate, and Dorothy rang it. A little man about the same size as the Munchkins appeared. He was clothed all in green from head to foot.

"I am the Guardian of the Gates. What is it you wish in the Emerald City?" he asked.

"We want to see the Wizard," said Dorothy.

The man seemed surprised at this answer. "It's been many years since anyone asked to see the Great Oz. I will take you to his palace, but you must first put on these green spectacles."

The Emerald City on the horizon

"Why must we wear spectacles?" asked Dorothy.

"Because if you did not wear them, the brightness of the Emerald City would blind you. Everyone in the city must wear spectacles day and night. Oz has ordered it."

The Guardian of the Gates opened a big box filled with spectacles of every size and shape, all of them with green glass. He put them on Dorothy and her friends, and even on Toto. Then he opened the gates and led them into the Emerald City.

Even with the spectacles on, Dorothy and her friends were dazzled by the brilliancy of the Emerald City. The pavement was made of blocks of green marble, joined together by rows of glittering emeralds. The streets were lined with beautiful houses of green marble, with window panes of green glass.

There were many people walking about, all dressed in green clothes. They looked at Dorothy with wondering eyes. There were charming shops with green candy, green popcorn, and green foods.

The friends were led to separate rooms where they could wash and rest before they saw the Wizard. Dorothy's room had a bed with green sheets and a green velvet cover. Her closet was filled with green dresses made of silk, satin, and velvet.

Inside the gates of Oz

The next morning after breakfast, a soldier with green whiskers came to fetch Dorothy. "The great Oz will grant you an audience. Your friends will also be granted an audience, but each of you will have to enter his presence alone," he said.

Dorothy put on one of the prettiest dresses from her closet. Then she boldly went to the throne room and looked around.

In the center of the room was a throne of green marble. An enormous head was floating over the throne. As Dorothy gazed in wonder, the head looked at her and said, "I am Oz the Great and Terrible. Who are you and why are you here?"

Dorothy took courage and said, "I am Dorothy, the Small and Meek. I want you to send me home to Kansas to my Aunt Em and Uncle Henry."

"If you wish me to send you home, you must do something for me. Kill the Wicked Witch of the West and I will send you home."

"But I cannot!" exclaimed Dorothy.

"That is my answer," said the Wizard. "Until the Wicked Witch dies you will not see your Uncle and Aunt again. Now go."

Sorrowfully, Dorothy left the throne room and went back to her friends.

Oz, the Great and Terrible

The next morning, the soldier with green whiskers brought the Scarecrow to the throne room. Inside was a lovely lady sitting on the throne. She was dressed in green silk and wore upon her flowing green locks a splendid crown. On her shoulders were silky wings. She looked upon him sweetly and said, "I am Oz, the Great and Terrible. Who are you and why do you seek me?"

The Scarecrow answered bravely, "I am only a Scarecrow, stuffed with straw. I come to you praying that you will put brains in my head, instead of straw."

"I never grant favors without return," said Oz, "but if you will kill the Wicked Witch of the West, I will give you brains. Until she is dead, I will not grant your wish. Now go and earn the brains you ask for."

The Scarecrow went back and told his friends what Oz said.

The next day the Tin Woodman went to see the Wizard. He found him in the form of a great animal, who gave him the same quest as Dorothy and the Scarecrow. When the Lion went the next day, Oz appeared as a great Ball of Fire. The Lion was also told that the Wicked Witch of the West must be dead before his wish would be granted.

The Scarecrow enters the great throne room

The friends took counsel together and decided that they would try to kill the Wicked Witch of the West. Therefore, the next day they left the Emerald City and traveled west.

Dorothy still wore the pretty silk dress that she had put on in the palace, but now, to her surprise, she found it was no longer green but pure white.

The Emerald City was soon left far behind. In the afternoon, Dorothy, Toto and the Lion lay down on the grass and fell asleep. The Woodman and the Scarecrow kept watch.

Now the Wicked Witch of the West had only one eye, but that eye was as powerful as a telescope, and could see everywhere. So, as she sat in the doorway of her castle, she happened to look around and saw Dorothy lying asleep, with her friends all about her. They were a long distance off, but the Wicked Witch was angry to find them in her country, so she blew a silver whistle that hung around her neck.

At once there came running to her from all directions a pack of great wolves. They had long legs and fierce eyes and sharp teeth. "Go to those people," said the Witch, "and tear them to pieces." The wolves dashed away at full speed.

The Wicked Witch of the West

The Scarecrow and Tin Woodman were awake and heard the wolves coming. "This is my fight," said the Woodman, and he seized his axe and slew the leader of the wolves. There were forty wolves and one after the other fell, until they all lay in a heap before him.

Dorothy was quite frightened when she woke up the next morning and found herself surrounded by a great pile of shaggy wolves, but the Tin Woodman told her all. She thanked him for saving them, after which they started again on their journey.

In the morning, the Witch came to her door and looked out with her far-seeing eye and saw her wolves lying dead. This made her angrier than before, so she blew on her silver whistle twice.

A great flock of wild crows came flying toward her, and the Witch said to the King Crow, "Fly at once to the strangers! Peck out their eyes, and tear them to pieces."

The wild crows flew in a great flock to Dorothy and her friends. The Scarecrow said, "This is my fight." The King Crow flew at the Scarecrow who caught it by the leg and killed it. There were forty crows and the Scarecrow killed each one until they all lay dead beside him.

The Scarecrow slays the crows

The Wicked Witch was angry when she saw her crows lying dead and she called a dozen of her slaves, the Winkies, and gave them sharp spears, telling them to go and destroy the strangers. The Winkies timidly marched away until they came to Dorothy and her friends. The Lion gave a great roar. The Winkies were terrified and ran back as fast as their legs could carry them. When they returned to the castle, the Witch beat them with a strap, and then sat down to consider what to do.

There was, in her cupboard, a Golden Cap, which had on it a magic charm. Whoever owned it could call three times upon the Winged Monkeys, who would obey any orders that were given. But no person could command these strange creatures more than three times. Twice already the Wicked Witch had used the charm of the Cap: once to make the Winkies her slaves and once to drive the Great Oz out of the West. She put the Cap on her head. There was a rushing of many wings, and the Winged Monkeys surrounded the Witch. "Go to the strangers within my land and destroy them all," she said, "except the Lion. I will harness him like a horse and make him work." The Winged Monkeys flew to the place where Dorothy and her friends were walking.

The Wicked Witch uses the charm of the Golden Cap

The Monkeys seized the Woodman and carried him over a country thickly covered with sharp rocks. There they dropped him on the rocks where he lay battered and dented. Then the Monkeys caught the Scarecrow and pulled all of the straw out of him. Other Monkeys threw stout pieces of rope around the Lion and flew away with him into the Witch's castle. There he was placed in a small courtyard with an iron fence around it.

The leader of the Winged Monkeys flew up to Dorothy, but stopped short when he saw the mark of the Good Witch's kiss. "We dare not harm this little girl," he said, "for she is protected by the power of good and that is greater than the power of evil." The Monkeys carried her to the Witch's castle.

The Wicked Witch was both surprised and worried when she saw the mark of the Good Witch's kiss on Dorothy. She looked down at Dorothy's feet and seeing the Silver Shoes began to tremble, but then she happened to look into Dorothy's eyes and saw that Dorothy did not know of the power of the shoes.

The Witch set Dorothy to work scrubbing the castle, often threatening to beat her. Dorothy worked very hard, for she was glad that the Witch had decided not to kill her.

The Wicked Witch threatens Dorothy

Now the Witch had a great longing to own the Silver Shoes, but Dorothy never took them off, except at night and when she took her bath. The Witch was too afraid of the dark to go into Dorothy's room at night, and she was even more afraid of water.

But the wicked creature was very cunning, and she finally thought of a trick to gain the silver slippers. Placing an iron bar in the middle of the floor, she turned it invisible to human eyes. Dorothy stumbled over the bar and one of her shoes came off. The Witch snatched it and placed it on her own skinny foot.

"Give me back my shoe!" demanded Dorothy. The Witch refused and Dorothy grew so angry that she picked up a bucket of water and dashed it over the Witch.

Instantly, the Witch gave a cry of fear and began to melt. "See what you've done!" she screamed. "In a minute I shall melt away! Didn't you know that water would be the end of me?" The Witch fell down in a brown, melted, shapeless mass.

Finally free, the Winkies proclaimed Dorothy a heroine and freed the Lion. Then they found and repaired the Woodman and Scarecrow. Dorothy took the magic Golden Cap, and summoned the Winged Monkeys to carry them back to the Emerald City.

Dorothy melts the Wicked Witch

When the four travelers arrived back at the Emerald City, they were brought in immediately to see the Wizard. Of course, each of them expected to see him in the shape that he had taken before, and all were greatly surprised when they looked around and found no one at all in the room. Suddenly, a voice, seeming to come from the top of the dome, said, "I am Oz, the Great and Terrible. Have you killed the Wicked Witch of the West?"

"Yes," said Dorothy, "we melted her."

"Come back tomorrow," the voice said. "I will think it over."

"You've had plenty of time already!" said the Woodman.

"We shan't wait a day longer," said the Scarecrow.

The Lion thought it might be as well to frighten the Wizard, so he gave a loud roar which was so fierce and dreadful that Toto jumped away in alarm, and tipped over a screen that stood in a corner. As it fell with a crash, they saw a little old man with a bald head who seemed as surprised as they were.

"Who are you?" asked the Tin Woodman.

"I am Oz, the Great and Terrible," said the little man in a trembling voice. "Please don't hurt me."

Toto discovers the secret of Oz

"Aren't you a Great Wizard?" asked Dorothy.

"No, my dear," he said, "I have been making believe. I have been a humbug. Please don't tell or I shall be ruined."

"What about my brains?" asked the Scarecrow.

"Or my heart?" asked the Woodman.

"Or my courage?" asked the Lion.

"How shall I ever get home?" asked Dorothy.

"If you come back tomorrow, I shall help you all," said Oz.

The next morning the Scarecrow entered the throne room. Oz filled his head with pins and needles. He cut a hole in the Woodman's breast and placed in it a small silk heart. The Lion he gave a potion he called courage. Then he turned to Dorothy.

"In order to go home," he said, "you must sew a big balloon out of silk. We will fill it with hot air to make it rise. It will carry us home, over the desert which surrounds us."

"Us?" asked Dorothy. "Are you going with me?"

"Yes," said the little man. "I am from Omaha myself. I came here in a balloon, and the people thought that I was a Wizard. I had them build the Emerald City, and I made everyone wear green spectacles, so that everything they saw looked green."

The Tin Woodman's heart

So Dorothy took a needle and thread, and as fast as Oz cut the strips of silk, Dorothy sewed them together. It took three days to sew all of the silk together, but when it was finished they had a bag of silk more than twenty feet long.

Then Oz painted it on the inside with a coat of thick glue to make it airtight, after which he announced that the balloon was finished. They fastened a big clothes basket onto it with many ropes, and when it was all ready, Oz sent word to his people that he was going to make a visit to his brother Wizards in the sky. The news spread rapidly through the city and everyone came to see the wonderful sight.

Before the balloon was to take off, Oz made a speech to the people, announcing that the Scarecrow would rule the city in his absence. Then he called for Dorothy.

"I can't find Toto," cried the little girl. She searched through the crowd for him and, at last, found him. She picked him up and ran toward the balloon.

When she was within a few steps of it, the ropes holding it down snapped. "Come back," she screamed.

"I can't," called Oz. "Good-bye!" The balloon floated away.

The balloon is launched

Dorothy wept bitterly at the passing of her hope to get home to Kansas again, but when she thought it over, she was glad that she had not gone up in the balloon.

The Scarecrow was now the ruler of the Emerald City, and although he was not a Wizard, the people were very proud of him. "For," they said, "there is not another city in the world ruled by a stuffed man."

The morning after the balloon went up, the four friends met in the big throne room to talk matters over. The Scarecrow sat on the throne and the others stood respectfully before him. The Scarecrow was thinking so hard that the pins and needles that Oz had given him for brains stuck out from all over his head.

"Let us send for the soldier with the green whiskers," he said finally, "and ask his advice on how to get Dorothy home."

"Glinda, the Good Witch of the South, might be able to help you home," said the soldier. But the road to the south is full of dangers to travelers. There is a race of strange fierce men who won't let anyone cross their country."

In spite of these dangers, the four travelers decided to seek Glinda's help in getting Dorothy home.

The soldier with the green whiskers

The sun shone brightly as our friends turned their faces toward the land of the South. They were all in the best of spirits and laughed and chatted together. Dorothy was once more filled with hopes of getting home, and the Woodman and Scarecrow were glad to be of use to her. As for the Lion, he whisked his tail from side to side in pure joy at being in the country again. They traveled all day and slept that night under the stars.

The next morning they came to a thick wood. The Scarecrow, who was in the lead, walked forward. Just as he came to the first tree, the branches bent down and twined around him. The next minute he was picked up and flung headlong among his fellow travelers. This did not hurt the Scarecrow, so he stood up and tried again. The trees immediately seized him and tossed him back.

"I believe I will try it next," said the Woodman. When a big branch bent down to seize him, the Woodman chopped it off with his axe. "Come on!" he shouted to the others. "Be quick!"

They all ran forward and passed underneath the trees without injury. The other trees of the forest did nothing to keep them back.

Attacked by the fighting trees

The four travelers walked with ease through the trees until they came to the furthest edge of the wood. Then, to their surprise, they found before them a high wall, which seemed to be made of white china. It was smooth, like the surface of a dish.

"I will make a ladder," said the Tin Woodman. While he worked, Dorothy and Toto lay down and slept for they were tired by the long walk.

After a time, the ladder was finished. The Scarecrow climbed up the ladder first, but he was so clumsy that Dorothy had to follow closely behind him to keep him from falling off. When they all arrived at the top of the wall, they were astonished to see a great stretch of country made entirely of china. There were pretty little barns and cows and chickens and pigs, but strangest of all were the people who lived in this queer country. There were milkmaids and shepherdesses, princes and princesses and funny clowns. The tallest of them came up to Dorothy's knee. Indeed, a funny little clown, all cracked, nodded saucily when Dorothy sat down to look at him. Dorothy and her friends traveled through the china country very carefully, for everything in it was very easily damaged.

Dorothy and the China Clown

They passed through the forest, and saw before them a steep hill, covered with rocks. The Scarecrow led the way and the others followed. They had nearly reached the first rock when they heard a rough voice cry out, "Keep back! This hill belongs to us and we don't allow anyone to cross it." Then, from behind a rock stepped the strangest man the travelers had ever seen. He was quite short and stout and had a big head which was flat at the top and supported by a thick neck full of wrinkles. He had no arms at all and seeing this, the Scarecrow did not fear that so helpless a creature could prevent them from climbing the hill.

"I am sorry," said the Scarecrow, "but we must pass over your hill," and he boldly walked forward.

As quick as lightning the man's head shot forward and his neck stretched out until the top of his head struck the Scarecrow and sent him tumbling down the hill. A chorus of boisterous laughter came from the other rocks where Dorothy saw hundreds of the armless Hammer-Heads, one behind every rock.

"We'll never get over this hill," she said.

"Why not call the Winged Monkeys?" suggested the Woodman. "You have the power to command them with the Cap."

The Hammer-Heads

Dorothy put on the Golden Cap of the Winged Monkeys and the monkeys promptly appeared. Dorothy asked the Winged Monkeys to carry them to Glinda's palace. The monkeys picked up the friends and flew away with them to the country of the South.

In front of Glinda's palace were three girls dressed in handsome red uniforms trimmed with gold braid. "We have come to see the Good Witch who rules here," Dorothy said. "Will you take us to see her?"

"I will ask Glinda if she will receive you," said a soldier girl, and went into the castle. After a few moments she came back to say that Dorothy and the others were to be admitted at once.

They followed the soldier girl into a big room where the witch Glinda sat upon a throne of rubies. She was both beautiful and young. Her hair was a rich red in color and fell in flowing ringlets over her shoulders. Her eyes were blue, and they looked kindly at the little girl. "What can I do for you, my child?"

Dorothy told her story, and finished by saying, "My greatest wish now is to get back to Kansas."

"I will send you back to Kansas," said Glinda, "but if I do, you must give me the Golden Cap."

Glinda's ruby throne room

"Willingly!" exclaimed Dorothy. "When you have it, you can command the Winged Monkeys three times."

"And I think I shall need them," answered Glinda, smiling. Then she turned to the Scarecrow, Tin Woodman and Lion. "What will you do after Dorothy has left us?" she asked.

"If I can get over the Hammer-Head's hill, I will return to the Emerald City, for I am their new ruler," said the Scarecrow.

"I would like to get back to the Winkies," said the Woodman, "for they have asked me to rule over them."

"Over the hill of the Hammer-Heads," said the Lion, "is a great forest. I should like to go there and live very happily."

"I shall command the Winged Monkeys to carry each of you to your homes. As for Dorothy, the Silver Shoes will carry her any place in the world in the wink of an eye."

"If that is so," said Dorothy joyfully, "I shall go home at once." She threw her arms around the Lion's neck and kissed him, patting his big head tenderly. Then she kissed the Tin Woodman who was weeping. But she hugged the soft body of the Scarecrow in her arms, and found that she was crying herself at the sorrowful parting from her loving comrades.

Dorothy says goodbye

Holding Toto closely, Dorothy clapped the heels of her shoes together, saying, "Take me home to Aunt Em."

Instantly, she was whirling through the air so swiftly that all she could see or feel was the wind whistling past her ears. Then she stopped so suddenly that she was rolled over in the grass several times before she knew where she was.

At length, however, she sat up and looked about her.

"Good gracious!" she cried.

For she was sitting on the broad Kansas prairie. Uncle Henry was milking the cows in the barnyard, and Toto had jumped out of her arms and was running toward the barn, barking joyously.

Dorothy stood up and found she was in her stocking feet. For the Silver Shoes had fallen off in her flight through the air and were lost forever in the desert.

Aunt Em had just come out of the house when she looked up and saw Dorothy running toward her. "My darling child," she cried, "where in the world did you come from?"

"From the Land of Oz," said Dorothy gravely. "And oh, Aunt Em, I'm so glad to be at home again!"

Home again

ABOUT THE ILLUSTRATOR

Greg Hildebrandt was born in Detroit, Michigan in 1939. Interested early in animation and special effects, he and his twin brother began their careers in animated and documentary films. In 1970, they moved into commercial and book illustration. Influenced heavily by N.C. Wyeth, Howard Pyle, and Maxfield Parrish, Greg and his brother quickly became successful illustrators and completed many mass-market and juvenile illustrated books. Proof of their success came in 1976, when they received the coveted Gold Medal from the Society of Illustrators. Greg and his brother then went on to illustrate three phenomenally successful J.R.R. Tolkien calendars, the famous "Star Wars" poster, and wrote and illustrated their first best-selling fantasy novel, "Urshurak". In 1983, Greg began his solo career by illustrating the classics. After completing "A Christmas Carol" and "Greg Hildebrandt's Favorite Fairy Tales" for Simon and Schuster, Greg began illustrating for this Unicorn line of classics and quality juvenile. So long as there are fairy tales and classics which warm the hearts of children of all ages, Greg Hildebrandt's brush will never be silent.